# For Abigail

PUFFIN BOOKS

Published by the Penguin Group
Penguin Books Ltd, 80 Strand, London WC2R 0RL, England
Penguin Putnam Inc., 375 Hudson Street, New York, New York 10014, USA
Penguin Books Australia Ltd, 250 Camberwell Road, Camberwell, Victoria 3124, Australia
Penguin Books Canada Ltd, 10 Alcorn Avenue, Toronto, Ontario, Canada M4V 3B2
Penguin Books India (P) Ltd, 11 Community Centre, Panchsheel Park, New Delhi – 110 017, India
Penguin Books (NZ) Ltd, Cnr Rosedale and Airborne Roads, Albany, Auckland, New Zealand
Penguin Books (South Africa) (Pty) Ltd, 24 Sturdee Avenue, Rosebank 2196, South Africa

Penguin Books Ltd, Registered Offices: 80 Strand, London WC2R 0RL, England

www.penguin.com

First published by Viking 2000
Published in Puffin Books 2001
3 5 7 9 10 8 6 4

Copyright © John Wallace, 2000
All rights reserved

The moral right of the author/illustrator has been asserted

Manufactured in China

British Library Cataloguing in Publication Data
A CIP catalogue record for this book is available from the British Library

ISBN 0-140-56652-X

# TINY Rabbit

## Goes to the Park

## John Wallace

PUFFIN BOOKS

Tiny Rabbit was excited. He was
going to the park with his friends.
First, Tiny Rabbit had to decide
what to take.

"I'll need my bag . . .

lots of carrots . . .

... my bucket
and spade, bat
and ball ...

some sun cream
and an anorak ...

me . . .

and, most
important of
all, Bunny."

Tiny Rabbit put
Bunny at the top
of his bag so he
could see out.

On the way, Tiny
Rabbit called for
his friend, Pig.

"I'll race you
to the park!"
said Tiny
Rabbit.

Tiny Rabbit's scooter was faster than Pig's bike, even though the wheels were smaller.

When they got to the park, Tiny Rabbit's friends were already there. "You stay here and watch, Bunny, while I go and play," said Tiny Rabbit.

Tiny Rabbit put on his sun cream . . .

got his bucket and spade . . .

and started to play.

Just then, he felt
a drop of rain.

Soon it was pouring.

It's a good job I brought my anorak,
thought Tiny Rabbit.
I'd better go and get it.

Tiny Rabbit was in such a rush that he didn't notice Bunny fall out of his bag and into the picnic hamper.

Tiny Rabbit put on his anorak. It certainly kept him dry.

When the sun came out again, all the friends ran off to the climbing frame.

I'd better check
Bunny's all right,
thought Tiny Rabbit.

But when he
looked in his
bag, Bunny
had gone!

"Oh no! Bunny's vanished!" cried
Tiny Rabbit.
"Don't worry," said Bear. "We will
all help look for him."

Pig looked in
the bushes.

Monkey looked
in the sandpit.

Bear looked in
the rubbish bins.

"Have you seen Tiny Rabbit's bunny?" Mouse asked the birds.

Cat even tried asking the ants. But Bunny had vanished.

Tiny Rabbit felt very sad . . .

"Have something to eat," said Pig.
"That always makes me feel better."

Pig began to look for something
tasty in the picnic hamper.
"Wait a minute!" he said ...

"What's this?
It's Bunny!
He must have
been in there
all the time!

Let's all celebrate with something to eat!"

Tiny Rabbit was delighted. He held on to Bunny extra tight . . .

*and* managed to help get the picnic ready.

"I don't want to lose you again, Bunny," he said . . .

"You're my best friend!"